Fiona French studied Art Education at Croydon College of Art
and went on to work as Bridget Riley's assistant. In 1970 she began
a distinguished career as a children's book illustrator and won the
1986 Kate Greenaway Medal for her book *Snow White in New York*.
Among her successful titles for Frances Lincoln are *Anancy and Mr Dry-Bone*,
winner of the Sheffield Book Award and selected for Children's Books of the Year;
Pepi and the Secret Names, written by Jill Paton Walsh, which was chosen
as one of Child Education's Best Story Books of 1994;
Lord of the Animals: *A Native American Creation Myth*, *Little Inchkin*
and *The Glass Garden*, written by Joyce Dunbar.
Fiona lives in Norfolk.

For Michael Da Costa

In 1883, the Rev. Lal Behari Day of Hooghly College in Bengal published *Folk-Tales of Bengal* (Macmillan and Co.), an anthology of traditional stories told to him by Bengali men and women in their native language. The collection included a story entitled 'The Match-Making Jackal'. This story was retold by Marcus Crouch under the title *'Siralu the Match-Maker'* in *The Ivory City – Stories from India and Pakistan* (Pelham Books, 1980). In Fiona French's retelling, the shrewd jackal has become Jamil's clever cat.

Hand-painted paper designs
by Dick Newby

First published in Great Britain in 1998 by Frances Lincoln Limited,
4 Torriano Mews, Torriano Avenue, London NW5 2RZ

First paperback edition 1999

British Library Cataloguing in Publication Data available on request

ISBN 0-7112-1209-0 hardback
ISBN 0-7112-1345-3 paperback

Printed in Hong Kong

3 5 7 9 8 6 4

FIONA FRENCH
with *Dick Newby*

JAMIL'S CLEVER CAT

A Folk Tale from Bengal

FRANCES LINCOLN

J amil the weaver lived on the poor side of town. He had a cat called Sardul, a very clever cat. Each night, while Jamil was asleep, Sardul wove material for his master to make into tunics and saris.

One morning, Jamil sighed, and said, "Oh Sardul, if only I could marry the princess who lives in the palace! Then you and I would not have to work our fingers and paws to the bone, and I would be a very happy man."

Sardul thought for a minute. Then he said, "Give me the best waistcoat and the most beautiful sari we have made, Master, and I will make your dream come true."

Sardul leapt silently over the roofs of the city, carrying the sari and waistcoat on his back. Looking down, he saw the princess in the palace garden.

Putting on the waistcoat, Sardul
sauntered into the garden and
bowed low, spreading out the sari.
"How beautiful!" exclaimed the
princess. Sardul bowed even lower.
"My master is the richest man
in the world," he said. "This is a
small token of his esteem."

The princess was
so flattered, she took
Sardul to meet her parents.
"Such a generous gift!" said
the Rajah. "Would your master
like to marry our daughter?"

"I think she would do very nicely," answered Sardul, and taking his leave, he went back to Jamil the weaver.

"We'll be rich," purred the cat. "The princess is eager to marry you. We must make you the finest wedding clothes ever seen."

They worked all night and all day and all the next night and day too. When Jamil tried on the clothes, he looked like a prince. Then Sardul invited some guests to the wedding...

He went out into the forest and gathered a wild chorus of creatures –

a roaring of tigers,

a chattering of monkeys,

a trumpeting of elephants.

What a noise they made on their way to the palace!

The animals hid among the trees in the palace garden – and the Rajah thought the noise was coming from a thousand people.

"We would be most honoured to meet the prince," the Rajah said, "but we have no room for all his retinue."

So Jamil and his cat went into the palace alone.

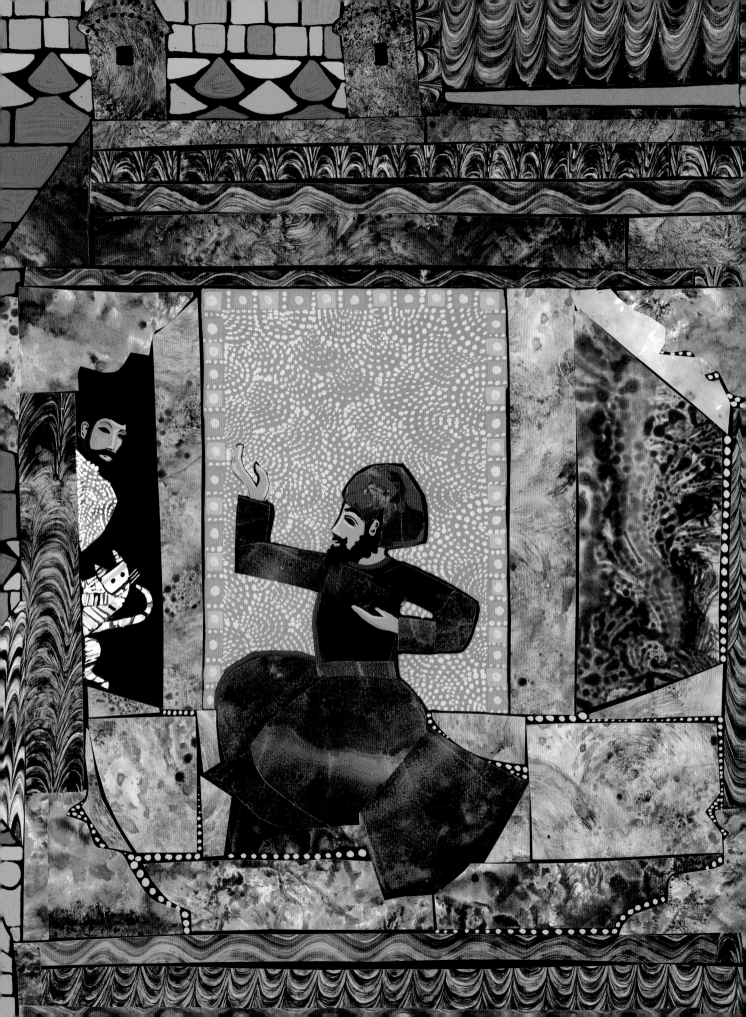

Next day, Jamil married
the princess.
    He looked so rich
and handsome – but
in truth, he was still
Jamil the weaver.

At their wedding feast,
he looked up at the
ceiling, and said,
"What a good place
to build a loom.
Those beams are
just right."

How strange,
thought the princess.
He seems to know
more about weaving
than ruling
a country.

Sardul said quickly,
"We must go. It is
time for my master
to welcome you
to his house."

When the princess saw her new home,
and Jamil confessed who he really was,
she was shocked – but not for long.
She loved Jamil the weaver as much as
Jamil the prince.

And so she became a weaver's wife. She was good at weaving too, after some practice. At the market, everyone wanted to buy her beautiful cloth.

Soon she could afford to hire helpers, and she and Jamil became rich. They built a fine new house and other weavers built homes around them. They all worked on the best looms money could buy.

When the Rajah and Ranee came to visit, they found the streets covered in silk, and were met by cheering crowds. Jamil and his wife welcomed them into their home.

"Did I not tell you the truth?" said Jamil's clever cat. "My master is the richest man in the world!"

MORE PICTURE BOOKS IN PAPERBACK
FROM FRANCES LINCOLN

LITTLE INCHKIN
Fiona French

Little Inchkin is only as big as a lotus flower, but he has the courage of a Samurai warrior.
How he proves his valour and wins the hand of a beautiful princess
is charmingly retold in this Tom Thumb legend of old Japan.

Suitable for National Curriculum English – Reading, Key Stages 1 and 2
Scottish Guidelines English Language – Reading, Levels B and C

ISBN 0-7112-0917-0

PEPI AND THE SECRET NAMES
Jill Paton Walsh
Illustrated by Fiona French

Pepi's father is commanded to decorate a splendid tomb for Prince Dhutmose,
with paintings of unimaginable creatures. Pepi decides to find his father
real-life models of the animals, using this knowledge of secret names...

Suitable for National Curriculum English – Reading, Key Stage 2; History, Key Stage 2
Scottish Guidelines English Language – Reading, Levels C and D; Environmental Studies, Levels C and D

ISBN 0-7112-1089-6

ANANCY AND MR DRY-BONE
Fiona French

Penniless Anancy and Mr Dry-Bone both want to marry Miss Louise,
but she wants to marry the man who can make her laugh. An original story,
based on characters from traditional Caribbean and West African folktales.

Suitable for National Curriculum English – Reading, Key Stages 1 and 2
Scottish Guidelines English Language – Reading, Levels A and B

ISBN 0-7112-0787-9

Frances Lincoln titles are available from all good bookshops.